The

GNU

and the

GURU

Go Behind the Beyond

———

A Cautionary Tale

PEGGY CLIFFORD

Illustrated by Eric von Schmidt

1970
HOUGHTON MIFFLIN COMPANY BOSTON

ACKNOWLEDGMENTS

To Juliana Forbes, aged ten, who offered constant advice, encouragement and inspiration in this undertaking.

To Magalen Bryant, aged forty, who kept insisting that gnus were noble and worthy beasts.

To Aubrey Burwell, aged seventy-two, who — if she did not actually invent the Behind-the-Beyond — was the first person to bring it to my attention.

To Judge and Mrs. William Shaw
whose wisdom, integrity, kindness
and spirit are proof enough
that there is much to be
hopeful about in this beset, nervous
and changing world

ONCE UPON A TIME, a graceful but hairy gnu was walking along, singing a song and smiling for no particular reason. On prancing around a very large rock, essaying an awkward two-step, he met a guru. The guru was very short and very fat. He was wearing a purple flower over his right ear and was all wrapped up in a lavender sheet. He had long black hair and a longer black beard. The gnu had never seen anyone quite like him.

The gnu said what he always said when he couldn't think of anything else to say. He said, "Hi."

"Hello," said the guru. "Are you, by any chance, a buffalo?"

"Good heavens, no! A buffalo is a kind of ox. I, on the other hand, am a member of the antelope family. I'm a gnu."

"You look more like a buffalo than an antelope," noted the guru.

"Everything's relative."

"What do you mean?"

"Well, that beard makes you look like a very old man.

7

On the other hand, your eyes have a youthful sparkle. Everything's relative."

"Hmmmm. Yes. For a gnu, you're very clever. Gurus are very clever, too," said the guru.

"What's a guru?"

Preening a little and standing very tall, the guru said, "I'm a guru."

"What's a guru?"

"What's a gnu? What are you?"

"I am what I am," said the gnu. "Whatever you see, that's what I am. There's no more to me than meets the eye."

"What do you do?"

"I eat. I sleep. I prance . . . but only occasionally. I butt trees with my great horns when I'm confused or angry. I roam. That's all."

"It sounds like a decent life," said the guru.

"It's adequate," said the gnu. "Now tell me about gurus."

"Well, it's a long story."

"I hate long stories," said the gnu.

"All right. I'll condense it, but you'll miss the best parts."

"I don't mind. It's been my experience that the best parts are usually vastly over-rated. Get on with it," said the gnu.

"You're terribly impatient, aren't you?"

"Yes. All gnus are impatient. It's one of our most prominent characteristics. We hate wasting time."

"Talking. Learning. That's not wasting time," said the guru.

"Doing is important. Talking isn't. Deeds not words. Besides, to be entirely honest, gnus aren't awfully good at talking. They are easily muddled. Their tongues tangle at the drop of a verb. Get on with it."

"Well, if that's the way you feel . . ."

"That's the way I feel."

"I'll put it as concisely as possible. A guru is a wise man. They have . . ."

"Who says so?" asked the gnu.

"Who says so what?"

"Who says that gurus are wise men?"

"Oh, I see," said the guru. "Well, they're chosen as children and then they are sent away to study with the wisest men in the land."

"Who says so?" asked the gnu again.

"Why do you keep saying 'who says so'?"

"Because I'm trying to get to the heart of the matter. You keep talking about wise men. I want to know who decides that they're wise. Do they look different from other men? Or what?"

"Yes. Gurus all wear flowing robes like the one I'm wearing. And they all have long hair and longer beards."

"But that's just a costume. Anyone can let his hair and beard grow and dress up in a sheet. I mean, I couldn't, but any man could. Wisdom doesn't come from costumes," said the gnu sternly.

"It isn't a sheet. It's a robe. A flowing robe."

"Call it whatever you like, it doesn't make you wise."

"Of course not. But only gurus dress this way."

"In other words, you decided to be a guru and you let your hair grow long and your beard grow longer and wrapped yourself up in that sheet — it is an attractive color, I must admit — and now you're a guru."

"No, there's more to it than that. I studied with the wise men and I have become very wise myself," said the guru.

"You're boasting."

"It's simply the truth," said the guru stuffily.

"If you're so wise, then tell me something strange and mysterious," challenged the gnu.

"That's not how it works."

"How does it work? That's what I'm trying to find out."

"I told you. I was chosen to study with the wise men and I have become wise myself."

"In other words, once upon a time someone decided that he was wise and he chose other wise men and they chose others and so on," said the guru.

"Yes. Exactly."

"That's ridiculous."

"I don't see why." The guru was now annoyed.

"Because to be wise, you have to be, well, special. From the beginning, you have to be a special kind of person."

"How do you know that I'm not a special kind of person?"

"Well, you do dress in a special way with those sheets and the flower in your ear and all, but, beyond that, you seem quite ordinary."

10

"You haven't given me a chance," pouted the guru.

"Special people say special things even when they're talking about the weather," snofled the gnu.

"I have a bicycle."

"A what?" said the gnu.

"A bicycle."

"What's a bicycle?"

"I'll show you."

The gnu followed the guru around the rock and there, leaning against the flat gray stone, sparkling in the sun, was the queerest thing he'd ever seen — aside from the guru himself, of course. It consisted of two great circles of shiny metal and many curves, arcs, twists, and straight lines. The gnu had no idea in the world what it did.

11

"That's the queerest thing I've ever seen. What does it do?" The gnu was careful to keep the guru between himself and the queer thing.

"It carries you around, takes you places, uphill and down again, anywhere you want to go."

The gnu gently butted the rock to clear his head. "How does it do all those things?"

The guru laughed. "I'll show you." Pulling his robe up around his knees, the guru got on the bike and pedaled rapidly away from the gnu.

It was an incredible sight. The guru went in circles and in straight lines. He turned easily this way and that. Finally, the guru skidded to a stop in front of the gnu.

"That's wonderful. In fact, it's amazing. But how do you keep your balance?"

"It's really very simple, once you get the hang of it. Would you like to try?"

"I could never do it," said the gnu. "I could never get the hang of it."

"Of course, you could."

"No!" said the gnu emphatically. Actually, he wanted very much to try, but he was afraid of falling, of failing.

"I have an idea! I'll drive and you can be my pas-

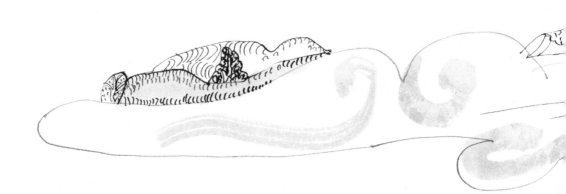

senger. Then you won't have to worry about falling."

The gnu decided that the guru was wiser than he looked. "But surely both of us will be too heavy for it. Surely, we'll break it."

"No, we won't. It's very sturdy."

Nervous and depressed, the gnu climbed onto the back slowly and said, "There's nothing to hold on to back here."

"Hold on to me."

"All right." He clutched on to the guru's robe.

"Are you ready?"

"Ready as I'll ever be," said the gnu sadly.

"Here we go. Don't drag your feet." The guru pushed off and away they went, sailing down the road.

It was, the gnu thought, a most peculiar feeling. He felt as if he were floating very rapidly over the ground. In spite of his fear, he rather liked it.

The guru turned around. "Do you like it? Fun, isn't it?" His hair and beard were streaming straight out in the wind.

"Keep your eye on the road!"

"Don't be nervous. I'm a terribly talented bike rider. I can even ride without hands."

"Don't do it now!" shouted the gnu, clutching more tightly on to the guru.

"Calm down," laughed the guru.

"I'll calm down, if you promise to keep your hands on the handlebars."

"All right."

"Promise?"

"Yes."

"Say it."

"I promise."

After a few minutes, the gnu relaxed and began to enjoy himself. It was a very unique way to travel. One sat still and moved all at once. And the scenery was quite attractive. Fields of daisies. Tall trees and small trees. Mountains in the distance. Blue sky. Green meadows. The gnu thought it was really quite marvelous.

"It's really quite marvelous, Guru."

"I told you so."

"Yes. You are wiser than I thought."

Suddenly, from below and behind them, the gnu and the guru heard a voice. "Hey! You almost ran over me!"

The guru skidded to a stop and the gnu almost fell off the bike.

"What was that?" said the gnu.

"Not what, WHO," said the voice.

The gnu stood up and bristled a little. He did not like voices which came out of nowhere.

The guru got off the bike and wheeled it to a tree where he leaned it, ever so deliberately. The gnu could see that the wise man didn't like to rush into things. The guru walked slowly back to the gnu and said, "Now what, or who, is speaking?"

"Me!"

The gnu and the guru looked all around.

"Down here!"

The gnu and the guru looked down and there, in the middle of the road, was a small gray mouse standing over a small blue bike.

"Oh, it's only you," said the gnu who was not always tactful.

"What do you mean, 'only you'? I may be smaller than you are, but that doesn't mean I'm less important," said the mouse.

The guru leaned down and smiled. "My, for a little creature, you're very brave. My friend didn't mean to insult you. It's simply his manner. He's very abrupt."

The mouse stood as tall as he could. "He's rude, too."

The gnu frowned and pawed the ground. "You're an unsavory creature, aren't you? Perhaps I'll step on you."

"If you do, I'll bite you with my magic teeth."

The gnu was astonished. "Magic teeth? What's magic about them?"

"If you step on me, you'll find out . . . to your everlasting sorrow," sneered the mouse.

The gnu turned to the guru. "You're a wise man, have you ever heard of magic teeth?"

"No. But wise men don't know everything. They know a lot, but not everything."

"What good are you, if you don't even know about essential things like magic teeth?"

"This is no time for a philosophical digression," said the guru.

The gnu trotted over to a tree and butted it with his great horns. "What on earth does that mean?"

"It means we should get on with it."

The gnu walked slowly back to the guru. "On with what?"

"On with our conversation with the mouse. He's brave, isn't he?"

"More foolish than brave, I'd say."

The mouse puffed his chest out. "A mouse with magic teeth is definitely not foolish."

The gnu snorted. "There he goes again . . . about those magic teeth."

The guru put his hand on the gnu's shoulder. "Calm down. You're much too excitable. Now, Mouse, what are you doing here in the middle of the road?"

"Ran over a pine needle. Had a flat tire."

The gnu laughed rudely, "Why don't you fix it with your magic teeth?"

The mouse roared, "I'll fix YOU with my magic teeth!" He ran at the gnu with teeth bared.

But the guru stepped between them. "Now, now. What an unpleasant way to act. Calm down, both of you. Now, how can we fix the tire?"

The gnu snorted sarcastically. "Why don't you give him a piece of your flowing robe to wrap around it?"

The guru said, "That's a wonderful idea."

"But," the gnu said, "I was only joking. I wasn't serious."

"Never mind. It's a splendid idea. I'll just tear a

piece off at the bottom where it won't show." And he did.

He picked up the little blue bike and wrapped the lavender cloth around the damaged tire.

The mouse said, "Why are you helping me?"

"Because you're a nice mouse," said the guru.

"Who said so?" said the mouse.

"I said so," smiled the guru.

"Well, you're wrong. I'm a wicked mouse and I'm selfish, too. And vicious. In fact, I guess that I'm about the nastiest mouse in the world." The mouse seemed very proud of himself.

"But you seem proud of it. Why does it please you so?" asked the guru patiently.

"To be noticed, you have to have a special quality. I'm mean — that's my special quality. Besides, it's fun."

"What a peculiar attitude you have," said the guru.

"Would you like to know where I'm going?" asked the mouse.

The gnu snorted, "No!"

But the guru smiled patiently and said, "Yes, of course, we'd like to know."

"Well, I'm not going to tell you."

The gnu tossed his head. "Guru, let him fix his own tire."

"No. When one can help, one should."

"Who said that?" asked the gnu.

"I did."

"I know that. But it has an important sound to it, as if someone famous had said it."

"Truth always sounds important," said the guru.

"Balderdash!" shouted the mouse.

The guru was very surprised. "What?"

"Balderdash! Lies or truth, it's all the same. It's not what you say, but the way that you say it."

The guru was now annoyed, too. "Don't you respect anything?"

"Myself. I respect myself."

The gnu said angrily, "Guru, there's no point in going on with this. That mouse is terrible."

The mouse smiled his nicest smile. "Don't you want to know where I'm going?"

The gnu said, "NO!"

"I'll tell you anyway. I'm going Behind-the-Beyond."

"WHAT?" said the gnu.

"WHERE?" said the guru.

The mouse laughed so hard that he fell down on the ground. "Ha-ha, Ho-ho, Hee-hee. I knew that would surprise you."

"What is it?" said the gnu.

"Where is it?" said the guru.

The mouse was still rolling gleefully around on the ground and laughing. "It's Behind-the-Beyond." He went on, rolling around and laughing.

"But what is it? Where is it?" said the guru.

"Behind-the-Beyond. That's what it is. That's where it is. Do you want to come with me?"

"Yes," said the guru.

"No," said the gnu.

"Yes, we do," said the guru.

"No, we don't," said the gnu.

"Why not?" said the guru. "Aren't you curious about the Behind-the-Beyond?"

"No. Besides, I'm on my way to France," said the gnu. He drew himself up and puffed out his chest, so as to look serious and important.

"What do you mean, you're on your way to France?" asked the guru.

"When I met you, I was just leaving," said the gnu.

"But that's silly," said the guru.

"It's ridiculous," added the mouse.

"It's not nearly as silly as going to the Behind-the-Beyond," said the gnu.

The mouse, finally through with laughing, stood up, dusted himself off, and said, "How do you know the Behind-the-Beyond is silly? You don't know what it is and you don't know where it is."

"Because it has a silly name. Whoever heard of anything called Behind-the-Beyond?" said the gnu.

"I did," said the mouse.

"Well, anyway, I'm going to France this afternoon. So obviously I can't go Behind-the-Beyond," said the gnu. Actually, he hadn't been on his way to France when he met the guru. He was going someday, of course. He thought about it frequently. He'd only mentioned it because he didn't want to go Behind-the-Beyond this afternoon.

"A trip to France costs a lot of money. A trip to the Behind-the-Beyond, on the other hand, is free," said the mouse.

The gnu hated to admit it, but the mouse had a point. But he said, "My financial affairs are not your concern, Mouse. I guess I'll be going now. It was nice to have met you, Guru. And I certainly enjoyed the ride. Goodbye."

"Please reconsider, Gnu. Going Behind-the-Beyond will be interesting and perhaps even exciting. Besides, as the mouse suggested, it's free."

The gnu paused. "Welllll, I suppose I could go to France next year."

"Of course, you could. Come with us. I promise you that it'll be an interesting trip," implored the guru.

"It'll be that, all right," muttered the mouse.

"What do you mean by that?" asked the gnu.

"Oh, nothing. Nothing at all," said the mouse. "Are you coming with us, or not?"

The gnu still wanted to be persuaded. "Welllll, I don't know."

"Come with us. Please!" said the guru.

The gnu smiled. "All right. After all, I wouldn't want to spoil your pleasure. How do we get there?"

The mouse said, "Blow up my tire and I'll take you there."

The gnu took the little bike from the guru and gave a huff and a puff and in a moment the tiny tire was fat and firm with air. He handed it down to the mouse.

The mouse got on his bike and said, "Shall we be off?"

"Yes," said the guru. "Is it a long trip?"

"Longer than some. Shorter than others. Let's go," said the mouse.

"Get on, Gnu," said the guru, as he wheeled the bike back onto the road and climbed on.

The gnu was still in a poor frame of mind. He neither liked nor trusted the mouse. He might be leading them into some sort of trap.

"How do we know that you aren't leading us into some sort of trap?" asked the gnu, as he climbed onto the bike behind the guru.

"Who on earth would want to trap a funny-looking man in a sheet and a moth-eaten gnu?" said the mouse.

The gnu began to sputter and storm, but the guru said, "Calm down. Calm down. That's only his way. Let's go, Mouse."

"Here we go," called the mouse, as he sped off down the road.

"Here we go," called the guru, as he sped after the mouse.

"I can't stand that mouse," muttered the gnu, as he clutched on to the guru's robe.

The two bikes with their mismatched passengers whirled through the countryside. It was a lovely day for a bike ride. Small, round clouds hung high in the sky which was as blue as the inside of a sapphire. The sun filled the air with a golden warmth and delicate fingers of wind toyed with the treetops. In the distance, a spangly river curled down a little hill and vanished behind a larger hill. The hillsides were rich and green, meadows divided by stands of tall trees. The travelers didn't meet anyone on the road.

They pedaled along for about an hour. Up and down hills, around curves, along stretches of road straight as a ruler. The gnu's temper was soothed by the rushing air. He even began to like the mouse who was pedaling at

a frantic pace to keep ahead of the guru. His tiny legs flashed round and round. As he bent over the handlebars, his long whiskers were swept back by the wind. The effect was quite rakish. The guru, too, was streamlined by the wind. His hair and beard flowed straight back and his robe whipped the gnu's knees.

The guru called out to the mouse, "I say, Mouse, how much farther is it?"

"You'll see. You'll see," shrieked the mouse.

"You know," said the gnu to the back of the guru's head, "there's something different about this country."

The guru looked around. The gnu was right. The blues and greens of the landscape had sharpened. The sky was suddenly bluer, the grass and trees greener. And there were vividly colored flowers everywhere. It was all quite dazzling.

"Is this it? Are we there?" called the guru to the mouse.

"No. Not yet."

The guru was disappointed. In his mind's eye, this was the way he had pictured the Behind-the-Beyond. Bright and beautiful. A kind of wonderland of color and sweet smells. Nature using its richest colors, its softest air, its very best of everything.

Suddenly, the gnu noted that, up ahead, shimmering on the road like a great round lightness was a cloud. It was not in the sky where it belonged, but on the road. It was a very odd and unsettling sight indeed.

"Stop, stop, Guru! There's a cloud on the road."

"Yes, I see it. Odd, isn't it? What do you suppose it's doing there?"

"I don't know. I don't care. I don't like it! STOP!"

The guru braked the bike to a stop.

The mouse squeaked his bike to a stop, too. "Why are you stopping?"

"There's a cloud on the road."

"Of course, there is," said the mouse.

"What do you mean, 'of course, there is'?" snorted the gnu.

"That's the way to the Behind-the-Beyond."

"Through a cloud?" asked the gnu incredulously.

"That cloud is the way to the Behind-the-Beyond?" asked the guru in amazement.

"Yes. Let's go," said the mouse.

The gnu said, "You mean we have to ride into that cloud?"

"Of course, we do. How else can we get to the Behind-the-Beyond?"

"I don't know," said the gnu, "but I definitely do not like the looks of that cloud."

"Why not?" asked the mouse.

"Well, for one thing, it's terribly pink. I mean, clouds are supposed to be white. For another, it's on the road. Clouds are supposed to be in the sky."

The mouse laughed unpleasantly. "Don't tell me that you are afraid of a cloud?"

The gnu snorted angrily. "Of course not. But it might be a trap."

"Are you coming?" The mouse snickered. "Or would you rather go to France?"

The gnu frowned at the mouse. "Why are you so consistently, so completely odious?"

"Because you are so consistently, so completely stupid," smiled the mouse.

"That's it. That is it! I've had enough!" shouted the gnu as he got off the bike.

But the guru restrained him. "Calm down, Gnu. He's trying to make you mad."

"No. He's not trying. He's succeeding. I'm going to squash him," said the gnu, lunging at the mouse.

The guru grabbed the gnu's ears. "Don't you want to go to the Behind-the-Beyond?"

"Yes, of course, I do," said the gnu. "But I don't like the looks of that cloud. And let go of my ears. That hurts."

The guru released the gnu's ears. "Sorry. Stop worrying about the cloud. It looks quite ordinary to me."

"But it's pink," said the gnu.

"Clouds are often pink. Haven't you ever seen a sunset?" asked the guru.

"Of course, I've seen a sunset. I've probably seen a million sunsets. But the sun isn't setting now. It's high up in the sky." The gnu gestured skyward.

"Besides, if it's so ordinary, what is that cloud doing on the road? Ordinary clouds stay in the sky where they belong."

"I guess it's a stray," said the guru.

The mouse spoke up impatiently. "That cloud has a reason for being on the road — a very good reason. Now are you coming or not?"

The guru looked at the gnu. "Shall we continue?"

"Yes. I guess so. But it's against my better judgment." He got back onto the bike.

The guru nodded to the mouse. "Lead on."

The mouse pedaled off, calling back, "There's no stopping now. We're committed. Follow me."

The two bikes with their three passengers sped down the road. As they approached the cloud, glistening pink and fat on the road, the gnu's throat got very tight and dry and his insides turned cold as stone. He looked around. It was unbearably beautiful. He didn't want to leave, but there was no stopping now.

The mouse whirled into the cloud and vanished. Then the guru and the gnu were suddenly inside the cloud, too. They couldn't see the mouse. In fact, they couldn't see anything. Suddenly, they heard a cry of pain and a terrible clattering.

"What was that?" said the gnu in a loud, high voice.

"I don't know," said the guru. At that moment, they crashed into something hard and cold. And the guru and gnu found themselves in a great tangle with the bike on the ground.

"I knew it! I knew it!" shouted the gnu as he untangled himself from the guru and the bike. "I knew this cloud was weird. Whoever heard of a hard cloud? Let's get out of here right now!"

Somewhere inside the cloud, the mouse laughed.
"Don't be silly, Gnu. You're a dunce. Someone simply
forgot to open the gate."

"What gate? Who forgot? What are you talking
about? What's going on anyway?"

The mouse's answer echoed back through the cloud.
"The gate to the Behind-the-Beyond. Somebody closed
it. I ran into it."

"Who closed it?" called the gnu.

"How should I know? They usually hear me coming
and open it. A closed gate can be dangerous in a cloud."
The mouse sounded annoyed.

The gnu turned to the guru. "What do you suppose
the gate is doing in this cloud anyway? I've never heard
of a cloud with a gate in it."

"It's plainly a very unusual cloud. The world is full of
mysteries."

"But doesn't a cloud with a gate in it seem, well,
unexpected?" said the gnu.

"Yes, but I rather like it," said the guru.

"Why?"

"I'm not sure. I like the surprise of it, I suppose. It's different."

"Yes, it certainly is different," said the gnu.

"Let's look for the mouse," said the guru.

"All right," answered the gnu.

Holding on to each other, they groped through the cloud. "It's awfully hard to see inside this cloud, isn't it?" asked the gnu.

"It certainly is."

"WATCH OUT!"

In fright and surprise, the gnu clutched on to the guru. "I knew we shouldn't have come. I knew it!"

"You're crazy, Gnu. You almost stepped on me, but you're upset. I'm the one who was almost squashed," shouted the mouse angrily.

The gnu looked down and there, between his hooves, was the mouse, looking — in spite of his small size — very fierce. "Oh, was that you?" he said.

The mouse puffed out his chest. "It was. And is. Only I almost wasn't. You came THAT close," he gestured with his paw, "THAT close to squashing me. Why don't you watch where you're going?"

"There's no point in watching when you can't see anything," sniffed the gnu. "I can't see anything inside this dumb cloud."

"Whatever else it is, it is not dumb. In fact, it's quite unique," answered the mouse.

"It may be unique. But that doesn't make it any easier to see through," said the gnu.

The guru intervened. "Calm down. Both of you. Gnu, the very nature of clouds makes them impossible to see through. That's one of the reasons they're called clouds."

The gnu frowned. "What are the other reasons?"

"I haven't time to go into it," said the guru. "Mouse, shall we get on with it?"

"We might as well. I called out for the gatekeeper. He should be here very soon."

"Maybe he's out to lunch," suggested the gnu.

"Impossible. Nobody in the Behind-the-Beyond eats lunch. In fact, there's no such thing as lunch," said the mouse.

"No such thing as lunch!" repeated the gnu. "Well, if you'd told me that I certainly wouldn't have come. I love lunch."

"Why don't they have lunch?" asked the guru.

"Because it's frivolous, unfunctional, and inefficient," replied the mouse.

"What mean things to say about something as lovely as lunch," said the gnu. "Who lives in the Behind-the-Beyond anyway?"

"You'll see. You'll see soon enough." The mouse laughed unpleasantly.

A ripple of fright ran down the gnu's spine. He did not like the mouse's tone of voice at all.

The mouse rattled the gate and cried out, "Gatekeeper, gatekeeper, I'm here. Let me in."

A moment later, a grizzled creature who seemed half-monkey, half-alligator, but was striped like a zebra, appeared at the gate. The gnu noted that while he was very old, he was extraordinarily orderly. There was something about him that was so tidy that he made the gnu feel uncomfortable.

He spoke. "Who goes there?"

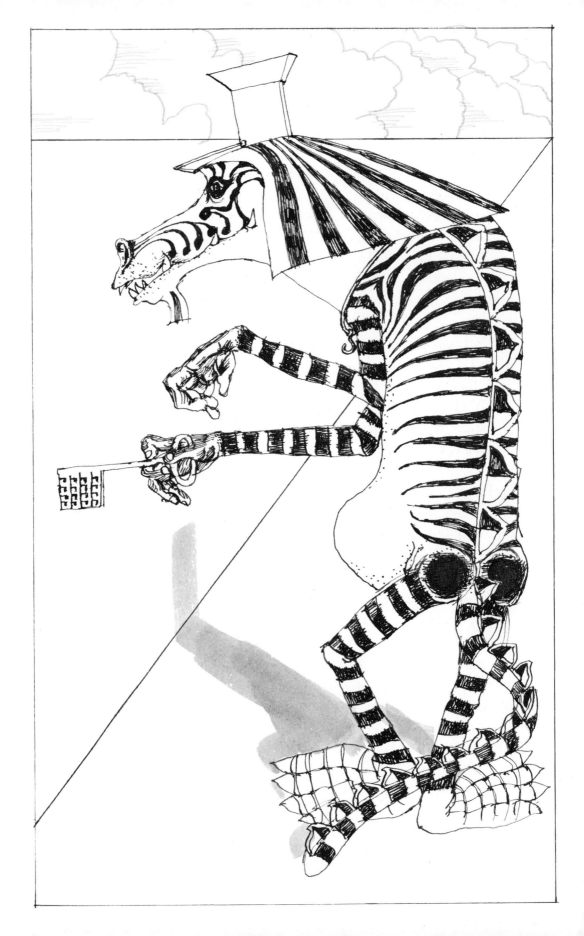

"Mouse," said the mouse.

The guru and the gnu were surprised when the gate-keeper responded warmly. "Oh, yes. Back again, are you? Whom did you bring for us this time?"

"A gnu and a guru," said the mouse. "Now let us in."

The gatekeeper unlocked the gate with a great golden key. He said, "I know something about gnus, but what's a guru?"

"A bearded man who wears sheets and goes about telling people how smart he is," said the mouse.

The guru was quite offended by this unflattering description and started to say something, but just then the gnu nudged him.

He said, "What did the gatekeeper mean, 'whom have you brought us this time?' That sounds very unpromising. In fact, it sounds quite menacing. Oh, I wish I'd gone to France."

Hearing the last part, the mouse chortled, "It's too late for that. Entirely too late. In you go."

"May I bring my bike in?" asked the guru.

"No. Leave it outside. Everyone travels by foot here. It's much more efficient," said the gatekeeper.

"But will it be safe?"

"Of course. The few creatures from the Outside who know the gate's whereabouts are entirely honorable. Like Mouse here," said the gatekeeper.

The gnu snorted. "If he's your idea of an honorable sort, we'd better bring the bike with us."

"NO!" said the gatekeeper. "You'd better learn to take orders. We believe in orders here. Giving them and obeying them without question. Is that clear?"

"Not entirely," said the gnu, nervously.

31

The gatekeeper grabbed him and pulled him through the gate. Then he grabbed the guru and pulled him in, too. Then he slammed the gate shut and locked it. "Welcome to the Behind-the-Beyond," he said.

Staring at him with very round eyes, the gnu said, "That wasn't a very nice welcome, Mr. Gatekeeper."

The mouse laughed. "You're frightened, aren't you?"

"Of course not," grumped the gnu, as he moved closer to the guru, which was silly as he was both smaller and weaker than the gnu.

Totally bewildered, the guru looked around. "My, it's quite unique. This Behind-the-Beyond."

The mouse said, "Is it what you expected?"

The guru looked around again. "Frankly, no. I mean, for example, I didn't expect the trees to be square."

The gnu looked around. The trees were square! And so were the bushes. The meadows were clipped as short as the fur around his hooves. There were lots of flowers, but they weren't ordinary flowers. Instead, they were triangles, hexagons, squares, and perfect circles. The sky looked freshly painted in very light blue.

"The sky looks freshly painted," he said.

"It is freshly painted," said the gatekeeper. "We paint it every morning. Otherwise, it gets streaked and shabby."

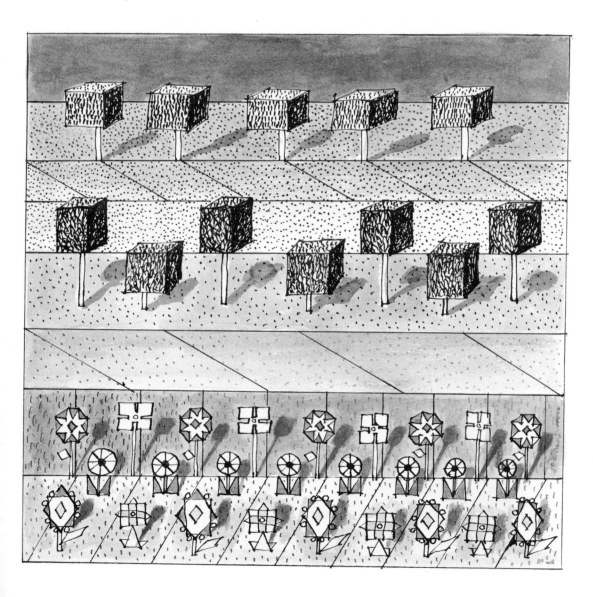

"I don't believe I've ever seen square trees and triangular flowers before," said the gnu.

"Ah," said the gatekeeper. "They weren't always that way. Some were bushy. Some were tall and thin as straws. Some were fat. We thought they were exceedingly messy. So we decided to make all the trees square and all the flowers geometrically satisfying. It makes for a tidier and more functional landscape, doesn't it?"

"Yes, it does," said the guru. "But don't you find it rather boring?"

"Order is never boring," said the gatekeeper.

' But," said the gnu, "you can't tell one tree from another. You can't tell them apart."

"So what? They're only trees," said the gatekeeper.

"Yes, that's true. Still, I do find it dull. I don't mean to be rude, but looking at all of those square trees makes me sleepy. And a painted sky! Whoever heard of a painted sky?" said the guru.

"The fact that you've never heard of it doesn't mean that it's not a good idea," said the gatekeeper. "Your sky gets streaked with gray and sometimes it clouds up. Messy! Messy, I say!"

"Perhaps," said the gnu. "But I've always been rather fond of our sky."

"Well, we're proud of our sky. Uniform. Our sky is absolutely uniform. We like that. Mouse, you'd better be on your way. They'll be waiting for you. You don't want to keep them waiting. You know how tardiness irritates them," warned the gatekeeper.

"Who?" asked the gnu nervously.

"Who?" asked the guru reasonably.

"You'll see," said the mouse. "Follow me. Goodbye,

34

Gatekeeper." The mouse set off down a great wide path which appeared to be made of glass, dark gray glass. The gnu and the guru — not knowing what else do to — followed behind. **1690195**

The gatekeeper called after them. "Remember, no littering. We're very stern with litterbugs. Very stern indeed."

"What does he mean by that?" asked the gnu.

"Drop something on the thruway and you'll find out," said the mouse ominously.

"What's a thruway?" asked the gnu.

"A thruway is a path which has been infinitely improved," explained the mouse.

"Well, this thruway appears to be made of glass," said the guru.

"It is," said the mouse. "They found that old-fashioned dirt paths were very impractical. When it rained, they rutted. They were bumpy. And, of course, they were impossible to keep clean. Glass doesn't rut, it's very smooth and, of course, it's quite easy to keep clean."

"But doesn't it break?" asked the gnu.

"I suppose it could be broken," said the mouse. "But things would go badly for anyone who broke the thruway. The citizens know that and, as a result, everyone is careful not to break it. That's one of the reasons that bicycles and other wheeled vehicles are not permitted. They might scratch the surface of the thruway."

"But wouldn't it be more convenient for everyone if they had ordinary paths and were permitted to ride bikes and other vehicles?" asked the guru.

"Convenience is nothing. Order is everything," said the mouse.

The guru's eyes went very round in his head. "If you don't mind my saying so, that's a very odd piece of reasoning."

"It's really none of your business, Guru. After all, you're only a guest here," said the mouse sternly.

"True. True. But it seems silly nonetheless," said the guru.

"I think so, too," said the gnu.

"I doubt that you think at all, Gnu," said the mouse merrily.

"What a horrid thing to say!" said the gnu.

"Perhaps. But true," said the mouse.

At that moment, they encountered a small band of the zebra-striped creatures. They were younger, more vigorous versions of the gatekeeper. Each one was carrying a tall, shiny spear and wearing what appeared to be a sparkling pot on his head.

The leader, who wore a white ribbon around his midsection, gestured and said to the mouse, "Are these the ones?"

"Yes," said the mouse.

"What does he mean, 'the ones'?" said the gnu nervously.

"Be quiet," said the leader. He turned to the mouse. "What are they?"

"The one in the sheet is a guru. The other one is a gnu," said the mouse.

"Funny-looking, aren't they?" said the leader. "They don't match at all."

All the other spear carriers laughed. But when the leader raised his spear, they all stopped laughing. Afraid as he was, the gnu couldn't help but admire their precision.

"What does he mean, 'they don't match'?" said the
gnu to no one in particular.

"We prefer matching pairs."

"For what?" asked the gnu. He had a feeling that
the meeting was going to end badly.

"You'll find out," said the leader. Raising his spear,
he shouted, "One, two, three, four, surround them."

The striped spear carriers made a circle around the
gnu and the guru. The mouse stood outside the circle
with the leader.

"What are you doing?" asked the gnu forlornly.

"Surrounding you, fool!" said the leader.

"I know that," said the gnu. "But why?"

"Who are you?" asked the guru.

The leader turned to the mouse. "You didn't tell
them?"

"No," said the mouse. "I like surprises."

The leader turned back to the gnu and the guru.
"We're the Ugga-Wuggas."

"The WHAT?" said the gnu and the guru together.

"The Ugga-Wuggas. Haven't you heard of us?"

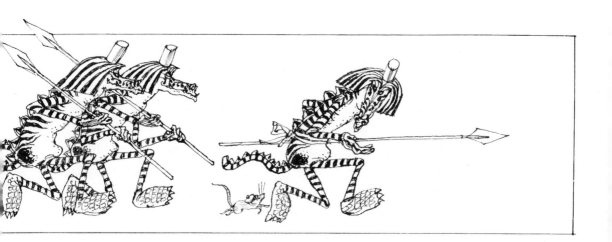

"No," said the gnu.

"That's too bad," said the leader. "I thought every-one had heard of us."

"Are you famous for something?" asked the gnu.

"Indeed we are," said the Ugga-Wugga leader.

"What is it?" said the gnu.

"You'll find out," said the leader. The gnu did not like his tone of voice at all.

"Well, come along," said the leader. He nodded to the spear carriers. "We're late, we'd better quick-step. I hate tardiness."

"Where are we going? What are we late for?" asked the gnu.

"Silence!" shouted the leader. He looked at the gnu and the guru thoughtfully. "I do wish you were a pair." He signaled the spear carriers who prodded the gnu and the guru into action. In a moment, they were all quick-stepping along the glass thruway. The mouse and the Ugga-Wugga leader took the lead, talking together as they jogged along side by side. The gnu wished that he could hear what they were saying.

In a few minutes, they came to a very large building. The gnu supposed it was a castle. Though it didn't have any of the usual castle decorations, it was most imposing. Like the trees and the bushes, it was absolutely square. And it was made of absolutely square, absolutely white stones. The Ugga-Wuggas and their prisoners quick-stepped right up to the big square door where they stopped on signal from the leader.

He raised his spear and called out, "One, two, three, four. One, two, three, four. One, two, three, four. One, two, three, four." Then he lowered his spear and stood in front of the door.

"What was that all about?" said the guru.

One of the spear carriers leaned forward. "The pass-word, silly. Four times four. Absolutely symmetrical. Beautiful, isn't it?"

The leader turned around. "Silence!"

The large square door swung open slowly and the troopers prodded the prisoners along into the castle courtyard. Then the door closed.

The gnu and the guru noticed immediately that all of the castle's interior walls matched. Windows. Doors. Arrangement of stones. Everything matched. Each of the upper left-hand windows had an orange towel hanging out of it. Stairs rose out of each corner of the courtyard and vanished inside the building. In the center of the courtyard was a square of grass and in the center of the square was a square flagpole which soared high into the air. At its top was a square flag whose design, of course, consisted entirely of squares. Four rows of four pink and orange squares. In the center of each of the sixteen squares was another smaller square of yellow. It was a surprisingly pretty flag, the guru

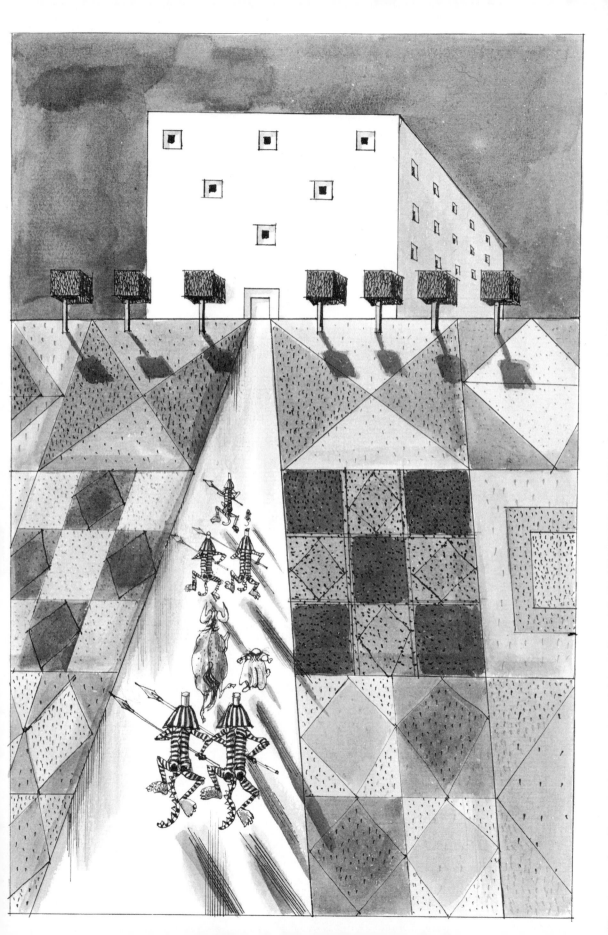

thought, but the beauty was in the colors, not the design. He decided that the design would probably make him quite dizzy if he looked at it for more than a moment.

There was something quite odd about the flag. At first, the guru couldn't figure out what it was. Then he had it. The flag — like the thruway — was made of glass. The guru nudged the gnu, who appeared to be quite undone by the events of the day. "The flag is made of glass," he said.

The leader whirled around. "Who spoke?" he asked.

In unpleasant unison, the spear carriers pointed at the guru and said, "Him."

The leader raised his spear. "What did you say?"

The guru said, "I said that your flag was made of glass."

"You find that odd?" asked the leader.

"Very," said the guru.

"Why?" asked the leader.

"Well, most flags are made of cloth. I've never seen a glass flag before."

"Glass is better for flags." The leader seemed very sure of himself.

"Why?"

"When the wind blows, cloth flags flap. When there is no wind, they hang limp. Wind or no, it's untidy. Our flag is always absolutely neat. It always looks exactly the same. Straight and square. You can always see the entire design. Besides, it's very easy to keep clean."

"Like the thruway?" asked the guru.

"Like the thruway," answered the leader. Raising

his spear again, he said, "Put the prisoners away. Mouse and I are going to have some tea and some talk. We have plans to make, things to discuss."

The spear carriers all raised their spears and began to lead the gnu and the guru away.

But the mouse stepped forward. "Leader, may I say goodbye to these silly creatures? It's not likely that we'll meet again." He laughed unpleasantly.

"Do you really have magic teeth?" asked the gnu.

"You'll never know now, will you? Goodbye." The mouse gestured to the spear carriers. "Take them away." And he walked toward the door with the Ugga-Wugga leader.

The spear carriers escorted their prisoners to the nearest staircase in double time. After quick-stepping up the steps, the gnu and the guru were quite out of breath. They were in a great hall. It was square, of course, and in each wall of the hall were four square doors. One of the spear carriers gestured to them. "This way," he said, "and be quick about it."

Suddenly it became painfully clear to the gnu and the guru that this wasn't a game. They actually were prisoners and they were actually going to be locked up in a cell. Somehow, until that point, the entire situation had seemed curious and frightening, but not disastrous. Now it seemed disastrous.

"You mean you're actually going to lock us up?" said the guru.

"Precisely," said one of the spear carriers.

"But why?" said the gnu sadly.

"Because you're our prisoners. The logical thing to do with prisoners is to put them in prison. You can see the logic of that, I'm sure."

"But we haven't done anything."

"That doesn't have anything to do with it. Prisoners must go to prison. It's really very simple."

"But we weren't prisoners until you captured us."

"That's beside the point. You're prisoners now. And, as I said, the only logical place for prisoners is prison."

"But it isn't fair," said the gnu.

"I don't know about that. All I know is that it's logical. Now over here. And be quick about it," said the spear carrier.

Within moments, the gnu and the guru found themselves locked up in the cell. It was quite mad, but there they were.

"It's quite mad," said the guru. "But here we are."

"But why?" said the gnu.

"You know as much as I know. You heard everything that I heard."

"I'm scared," said the gnu. "And I don't care who knows it."

"So am I. Nothing in my life has prepared me for this."

"Who do you suppose the Ugga-Wuggas are?"

A spear carrier answered through the little window in the cell door. "Ugga-Wuggas are Ugga-Wuggas. We rule the Behind-the-Beyond. That's all there is to that."

"But why have you captured us?" asked the guru.

"It's very simple."

"Not to us. Please explain."

"Well, several eons ago, we conquered the Behind-the-Beyond. Its previous residents had gotten it in a terrible mess. Bushy bushes. Flowers everywhere. Frequent rainstorms. Occasional rainbows. Meadows full of tall grass. It was, in a word, very untidy. Well, we straightened it out in short order. Made the bushes and the trees square. Painted the sky. Harnessed the clouds to do our bidding. Regulated the rain so that it came at regular intervals. Banished the rainbows. Trimmed the meadows. Built the thruway. After we'd done all that, we had very little to do. So we decided to take prisoners."

"But surely," said the guru, "there were other things you could have done. Stamp collecting is very worthwhile, I understand."

"Perhaps. But taking prisoners is infinitely more worthwhile," said the spear carrier.

"For any particular reason?" asked the gnu.

"For two particular reasons. First, it gives us something constructive to do with our time. Second, we had all of these prison cells, and prison cells are simply not complete without prisoners. You can understand that. So our current project is filling the prison cells. Two to a cell. Preferably matched," said the spear carrier.

"We're not matched," said the guru.

"I know. That is unfortunate," said the spear carrier.

"And what role does the mouse play in all of this?" asked the gnu.

"He's what you might call a bounty hunter. We can't go beyond the gate. And so we pay him to bring us prisoners to put in our cells. He's very clever, you know, but he didn't do a very good job with you."

"What do you mean?" asked the gnu.

"Well, we're very partial to pairs. And, as I said, you two are obviously not a pair. You don't match at all. You don't really fit in."

"We'd be happy to leave," said the gnu eagerly.

"No. A mismatched pair is better than no pair at all. A full cell is better than an empty one."

"What will happen to us?" asked the gnu.

"Nothing, I imagine. You'll live in the cell. We'll feed you and take you for occasional walks. That's all," said the spear carrier.

"How long will this go on?" asked the guru.

"Forever," said the spear carrier. "Goodbye." He vanished.

The gnu and the guru stared at each other in amazement.

"Forever?" asked the gnu. "That's a long time."

"Forever!" replied the guru.

"But I don't want to stay here forever. I have things to do, places to go," said the gnu.

"Perhaps he was joking," replied the guru.

"Did he look like he was joking?" asked the gnu.

"No," said the guru.

"I have the feeling that Ugga-Wuggas don't joke. You know, I hate to be an I-told-you-so, but I never trusted that mouse. Imagine! A bounty hunter!" said the gnu.

"I know. I feel quite badly about that," said the guru. "After all, I talked you into coming along. I should have let you go on your way to France."

The gnu blushed. "I'd never have gotten there."

"Probably not. But you wouldn't have ended up

here either." The guru looked quite unhappy.

"That's true. I have to agree. But there's no use crying over spilt tea."

"Milk."

"What?"

"It's spilt milk that you shouldn't cry over."

"Well, no matter. A little of either would taste very good right now. What shall we do?" said the gnu.

The guru looked around the cell sadly. "I don't know. For once in my life, I don't know what to do. I'm so disappointed in that mouse."

"Forget the mouse. What will we do?"

"Let me think." The guru walked over to an orange chair and sat down. He landed on the floor. "What happened? What's going on? Was there an earthquake? What?"

The gnu helped the guru to his feet. "I don't know. You sat on the chair and fell on the floor." He looked closely at the chair. "There's something odd about this chair." He reached out and touched it. "It's not a chair at all! It's a picture of a chair! A picture of a chair painted on the wall. Isn't that extraordinary? Come sit on the bed." The gnu led the guru to the bed and helped him down onto it. Again, the guru fell on the floor.

"It happened again," said the guru sadly. "I sat down and fell on the floor again."

"Good grief!" said the gnu. "The bed's only a picture, too." He raced around the cell, touching all of the furniture. It was all painted on the wall. The chair. The two beds. The table. All were pictures. Even the curtains at the barred window were painted on the wall. "All of this furniture is a joke."

Getting up off the floor, rubbing his back, the guru said, "Well, it's a very bad joke. The floor is hard!"

"It's like the sky!" exclaimed the gnu.

"What do you mean?"

"Don't you remember? The sky is painted, too. I guess the Ugga-Wuggas think that painted furniture is neater than real furniture," said the gnu.

"It may be neater, but it's not nearly as comfortable," sighed the guru. "We have to get out of here. The painted furniture is the last straw. The straw that broke the camel's back."

"But you're not a camel. At least you don't look like a camel. If you're a camel, you're wearing an awfully clever disguise. Why, I can't even see your humps," chattered the gnu.

"Don't be silly. Of course, I'm not a camel. That's an expression. It means 'I've had enough.'"

"Good. So have I. Let's escape."

"But how?"

"Maybe we can take the guard by surprise," suggested the gnu.

"What guard?"

"I don't know. There must be guards here. You can't have a really good prison without guards. And when our guard comes in, we'll take him by surprise and escape. People are always doing that in books," said the gnu.

"All right. But even if we manage to escape from the cell, how will we get out of the castle? And if we're lucky enough to get out of the castle, how will we get out of the Behind-the-Beyond?" asked the guru.

"First things first. After we take the guard by surprise, we can worry about the rest of it."

"I don't think it'll work," said the guru.

"Maybe not. We'll just have to try and hope for the best."

"All right. But it's hard."

"What?" asked the gnu.

"Hoping for the best when you're locked up in a cell with painted furniture in a strange castle in a strange land," sighed the guru. "What's that noise?"

They listened to a clang of glass.

"Ah, they're probably bringing our dinner. Are you ready?" asked the gnu excitedly.

"For what?" asked the guru.

"To take the guard by surprise," replied the gnu.

"As ready as I'll ever be." The guru was not fond of violence, partially because he disliked the idea of fighting and partially because he was not good at it. In fact, he had never in his life won a fight.

A guard, who looked remarkably like the leader, peered through the little window in the door. "I have your dinner," he said.

"Fine. Fine," said the guru. "Bring it right in."

"No. You come and get it. I'm a guard, not a waiter," muttered the guard. "Besides, three's a crowd and crowds are untidy. You should know that."

Eying the gnu, the guru said, "Yes, that was silly of me."

"Well, come and get it. I haven't got all night. I have better things to do than stand around talking to you," said the guard.

The guru went over to the door and the guard handed two glass bowls through the little window. The guru took the bowls and looked at the food — perfect squares of bread in crystal clear water.

"Bread and water! Is that our dinner? Is that all?"

"What did you expect? Artichokes and chicken fricassee? You're only prisoners, you know. And mismatched prisoners at that." The guard vanished.

The guru handed one of the bowls to the gnu. "Well, that rules out taking the guard by surprise, I guess."

"Yes. It would be difficult to overpower him through the door," said the gnu.

"Bread and water makes everything more difficult," sighed the guru.

The gnu sighed, too, and gulped his dinner down in one great swallow. "No taste. No taste at all." He put the bowl down on the floor, in front of the painted table.

"Well, if we can't overpower the guard there's only one alternative," said the guru.

"What's that?" asked the gnu.

"The window. If we can't go out through the door, we'll have to go out through the window."

The gnu looked at the window thoughtfully. "But it's barred."

"Maybe we can bend the bars."

"Unlikely," said the gnu.

"But we have to try," said the guru.

"You're right. We have to try. Why don't you climb up on my back and look at them more closely?" He moved under the window. "Climb on," he said to guru.

The guru climbed up onto the gnu's back and pressed his face close to the window.

"What do you see?"

"A lot of square trees and bushes," answered the guru.

"No, I'm talking about the bars."

"Well, I see the bars. They appear to be very thick."

"That's bad news," said the gnu.

"But, wait! Wait!"

"I'm not going anywhere," said the gnu.

"The bars . . . they're like the furniture. They're painted. They're painted on glass."

The gnu whirled around and leapt up to see for himself, flinging the guru to the floor. "Let me see! Let me see!" Then, noticing the guru in a heap on the floor, he said, "Oh, I'm sorry. I am sorry. I forgot about you in my excitement. Let me help you up."

The guru groaned. "I believe the floor is getting harder." He got slowly to his feet. "Oh my, I have a terrible backache."

"I'm sorry. I really am very sorry, Guru. Is there anything I can do for you?"

The guru was leaning against the wall, clucking to himself. "Yes. You can get me out of here before I break in two."

"Yes. Yes. All right. You just relax. I'll have you out of here in no time."

"It's not that I mind the pain, you know, it's simply that it's so, well, undignified for a guru to keep falling on the floor."

"But it's not your fault. It really isn't."

"Thank you. It's nice of you to say so. But I feel foolish anyway. Gurus are simply not supposed to go around falling down all the time."

"Well, I think that you are a grand guru. Now I'll have a look at this window." He stood up on his hind legs and looked at the window. Indeed, it was all glass and the bars were made of nothing more than paint. "I think that the thing to do is break the window — and the bars — and leave this odious place. It'll be very simple."

"Suppose the guard hears the glass breaking?" said the guru.

"Yes," said the gnu. "That wouldn't do at all." He thought for a moment. "I have it! We'll sing to cover the noise."

"But I have a terrible singing voice," said the guru.

"Please, Guru, we can't be fussy at a time like this. We have to sing . . . unless you want to stay here with the painted furniture and bread and water and unpleasant guards. Call the guard. Tell him that we're going to sing. Tell him that gurus always sing at dusk."

"But they don't. They rarely sing. And I never sing because, as I said, my voice is simply awful," said the guru.

"Never mind. Never mind. Just call him," said the gnu.

The guru limped to the door and called out, "Guard! Oh, Mr. Guard."

In a minute, the guard's face appeared at the window in the door. He looked angry. "Yes. What is it? What's all the shouting about?"

"Well, first, I'd like to return the dishes to you." He scurried around, gathering up the dishes. "Here they are. And thank you for that delicious supper."

"It wasn't delicious. You can't fool me. It had no taste at all. But it was neat. Absolutely square pieces of bread in absolutely crystal clear water. It has a beauty all its own. Now go to sleep. It's sundown. Stretch out on the beds. They're very comfortable." He laughed unpleasantly.

"Yes," said the guru. "We tried them."

The guard laughed again. "Oh, good. Good! Did you hurt yourselves?"

"Yes I did, as a matter of fact. Why are they painted on the walls? Why don't you have real beds and chairs and tables in the cells?"

"Because real furniture is expensive. And it's a bother. It gets broken and collects dust. We hate dust. It isn't functional," said the guard.

"That's what we deduced," said the guru.

"Why did you ask me about it then?"

"To verify our opinion," said the guru.

"What?"

"Unverified opinions are not functional," said the guru.

The guard looked confused. But he said, "Oh, yes, of course. Well, I must get back to my post. Go to sleep. It's sundown."

"That's the other thing," said the guru.

"What other thing?"

"The other thing I wanted to tell you. I, as you may know, am a guru and . . ."

"I don't know what you are or aren't. I only know that you don't match him. We don't like that," said the guard.

"I know. I'm sorry about that. But, in any case, I am a guru and we always sing a guru song at dusk."

"Guru song? What on earth is a guru song?" asked the guard nervously.

It was obvious, thought the gnu, who was standing ever so casually by the window, that the guard had no imagination at all. Imagination was probably forbidden.

"Well, it's hard to explain," said the guru. "But it's a very important part of my life. If I can't sing my song, then I can't go to sleep."

"Is he going to sing with you?" asked the guard.

"Yes. He has graciously consented to sing along with me, even though he's a gnu."

"A what?"

"A gnu."

"Guru. Gnu. It all sounds the same to me," said the guard in some confusion.

"But it isn't. You said so yourself. We aren't a matched pair."

"Yes, I did say that myself. I remember it well. Just a moment ago, I said that very thing." The guard seemed unaccountably upset. "Well, go ahead. Sing your whatever-you-call-it. But sing quietly. The other prisoners are trying to sleep. Besides, noise isn't. . ."

"I know," said the guru. "Noise isn't functional."

"Right. And if your song lasts for more than five minutes, I'll have to take steps."

"What steps?"

"You'll find out, if you sing for more than five minutes. Remember what I said. Not too loud and not long." The guard left with the two glass bowls.

The guru peered through the window in the door. "He's gone. What shall we sing?"

"Do you know 'Shine On, Shine On, Harvest Moon'?"

"No."

"Too bad. It's very pleasant to listen to. All right. Just make something up. I'll join in," said the gnu.

The guru thought for a minute and then began to sing.

> I wish I were back at home,
> where only the gnus roam,
> where the fish are fat and sleek
> and Sunday lasts all week,
> I wish I were back at home.

The gnu, with tears in his eyes, said, "That's a terribly nice song and I think you have a splendid voice."

The guru blushed. "It's nothing. Join me in a chorus or two. And break the window when we get to the part about the fish."

They sang together and when they reached the part about the fish, the gnu smashed the window with his hoof. He whispered to the guru, "Be careful of the glass. I'm going to look out the window and see what I can see." He stuck his head out the window. In a moment, he pulled his head back in. "We forgot one very important thing."

"What's that?"

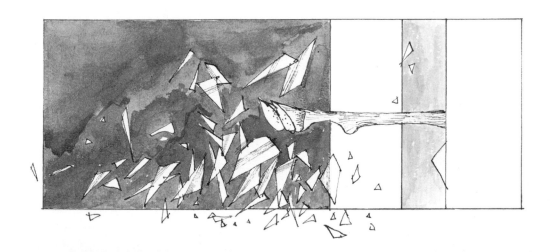

"We're on the second floor." The gnu leaned against the wall and moaned quietly.

The guru moaned back. "I completely forgot about that. What can we do?"

"Well, gnus are extraordinarily good jumpers. I mean, I could probably jump out of the window and into a bush without harm. But you can't."

"No, I can't. I'd break. Perhaps we can make a ladder," suggested the guru.

"There's nothing here to make a ladder out of. All the furniture is painted on the walls. There isn't so much as a scrap of wood or anything else useful in this cell."

"That's true unfortunately," sighed the guru. "If we only had a piece of rope. . ."

"Yes, a piece of rope would be lovely." The gnu scratched his head. "But wait, WAIT! We have your robes." He studied the guru thoughtfully. "Yes. Yes! They'll be fine. Undress. Undress quickly. Then we'll lower the length of cloth out the window and you can simply slide down to earth."

"But my lovely robes. . ."

"This is no time for sentiment. Quick!"

Still, the guru hesitated.

The gnu spoke sternly. "Which would you rather have? Your lovely robe or your freedom? Anyway, if we're careful, we can put it back together again and it'll be as good as new . . . or almost as good as new."

"Yes. You're right, my friend. I'm being unduly sentimental." Sadly, slowly, the guru unwrapped his robe. It was an immensely long piece of material. Underneath was another piece of a slightly lighter shade of lavender. "It's terribly embarrassing, you know."

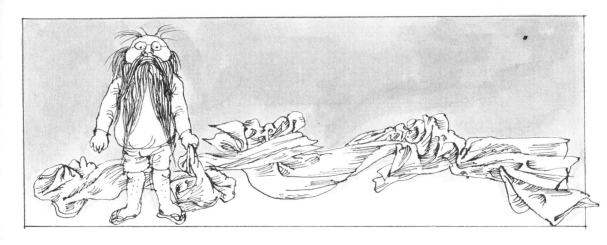

"It'll all be over in a minute. But you must hurry."

Underneath all of the lavender, the guru was wearing a cotton shirt and shorts. He was considerably thinner without his robes.

"You're not nearly as fat as I had thought you were," said the gnu.

"I'll thank you to keep your opinions to yourself. Without my robes, I don't even feel like a guru. Oh, my lovely robes. I hope we don't rip them," muttered the guru.

"You must make sacrifices for freedom," said the gnu pompously. "Hand them over. I'll drop them out the window."

The guru gave the gnu his robes and the gnu, after making sure that there was no one outside, dropped the robes out the window, having knotted them together. "Now, up on my back and down the robes! Quick! The way is clear, but it's getting dark."

The guru did as he was told and, in a moment, was safe on the ground below. The gnu tossed down the robes and the guru immediately began wrapping them around himself. Up above, the gnu's head came out the window. "Here I come," he called. Flying through the air with no little grace, he landed squarely in one of the square bushes. The guru rushed over to him.

"Are you all right, Gnu?"

Climbing out of the bush, the gnu said, "I think so. Now we must get away from here immediately. Which way shall we go?"

Making some final adjustments on his costume, the guru said, "I think we should creep around the castle until we come to the thruway, then we should follow it to the gate."

"That seems sensible enough," said the gnu. "Let's go. But be very quiet. Whispering and tiptoeing are in order here."

Whispering and tiptoeing, they circled the castle three times without finding the thruway.

"This is ridiculous," said the gnu. "We came here on the thruway. It has to be here somewhere."

"Maybe they roll it up at night," joked the guru.

"That's it! That's it!" said the gnu.

"I was only joking. A small joke."

"No, you're right. I saw a big roll of glass back there. They do roll the thruway up at night."

"But that's silly," said the guru.

"This entire place is silly. Nothing makes sense here. And you know how they feel about order. They probably think that an unused thruway is unfunctional."

"So at night they roll it up?"

"Right! Over here." The gnu tiptoed quickly to the great roll of thruway.

Following him, the guru whispered, "The Ugga-

Wuggas are very peculiar, VERY peculiar." He looked over the gnu's shoulder and, indeed, there was the thruway, all rolled up like Christmas ribbon.

"Shall we unroll it?" asked the guru.

"No," said the gnu. "I'm afraid that it would make a terrific clatter. Besides, when the Ugga-Wuggas saw the thruway unrolled, they would know we'd escaped. And, besides that, we might break it. And then there's no telling what they might do to us." He shuddered.

"I guess you're right. We'd better just walk out in this direction. Actually, if we walk in a straight line away from the castle, we should be able to find the cloud without the thruway anyway," said the guru.

"Well, let's go. I'd really like to be far, far away by morning," said the gnu.

And the gnu and the guru set out across the smoothly trimmed meadows. Behind them, the castle got smaller and smaller and finally was swallowed up in the dark. In front of them, the Behind-the-Beyond stretched out forever. Or so it seemed. The square bushes and trees and the smooth meadows were pleasant enough to stroll through, being soft underfoot and quiet, but there was a terrible sameness. It was, on the whole, very boring.

"It certainly is boring," said the gnu. "If we weren't on the run, I'd fall asleep from the sheer boredom of it all."

"It is boring," agreed the guru. "But it's awfully kempt. I've never seen anyplace so kempt in my life."

"Kempt?" Is that a word?"

"Of course. You've undoubtedly heard of unkempt?"

"To be honest, I haven't," said the gnu.

"Well, anyway, kempt is the opposite of unkempt."

"And what's unkempt?"

"Disorderly. Messy. Untidy."

"All the things the Ugga-Wuggas can't stand. Then kempt must mean orderly, tidy, unmessy. All the things the Ugga-Wuggas worship." Looking around, the gnu added, "Yes, I'd have to agree. It is certainly kempt." He scratched his head thoughtfully, as they walked along. Suddenly, he shouted, "Look over there! Quick!"

The guru said, "What? Where?"

"Over there. That cloud. That must be the cloud with the gate in it. Quick! Quick!"

"Wait, Gnu. We must have a plan. We can't simply charge into the cloud. Remember the gatekeeper."

"Maybe we can take him by surprise."

"Yes," said the guru. "We'll sneak up quietly and pounce on him and open the gate and be on our way home in a flash."

"That won't work," said the gnu sourly.

"Why?"

"Because it's impossible to see inside the cloud."

"That's true. But what else can we do?" asked the guru.

"Nothing I guess. Let's go," replied the gnu.

Slowly and quietly, they crept up to the cloud. They didn't make a sound. The cloud was as quiet as they were. The guru waved to the gnu. They pounced. And landed on top of each other inside the cloud.

"I knew it wouldn't work," whispered the gnu.

"It'll work. It'll work. We'll just keep pouncing until we find the gatekeeper," said the guru.

"If you say so," said the gnu, as he pounced again. There, right in front of him, was another gnu. Precisely his age and size. It was an amazing coincidence. He walked up to him confidently and said, "How did you get here? Never mind. I'm delighted to see you."

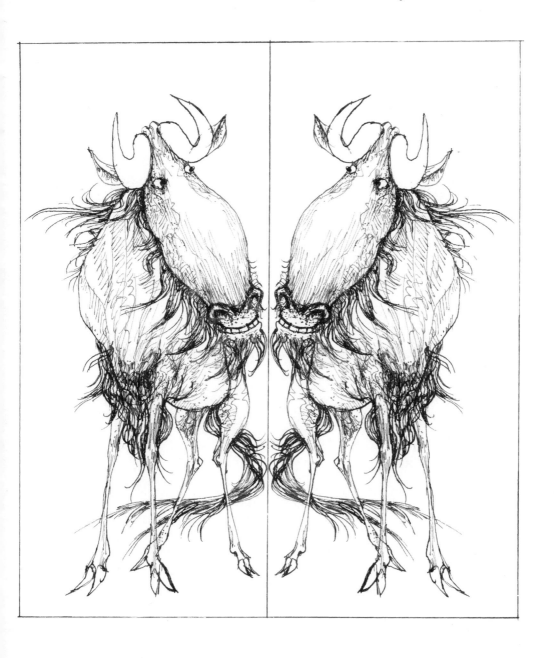

The other gnu appeared to be talking, but the first gnu couldn't hear what he was saying. He looked very friendly, however, which was only natural as gnus are fonder of other gnus than anyone else on earth. Just then, the guru pounced out from somewhere and, suddenly, standing right beside the other gnu was another guru.

"This is an astonishing coincidence, Guru. I was standing here, having a most enjoyable conversation with this other gnu and then you came along and now there's another guru, too. It is astonishing. Two new friends, allies who, by the most amazing turn of luck, are just like us. Why. . ."

"Stop babbling, Gnu. That's a mirror. You're looking at us in a mirror."

All at once, the gnu felt foolish and sad. He wanted to cry. He had been so happy to see the other gnu. It had been such a wonderful surprise. But it was only a mirror. He had been talking to himself in a mirror. Oh, he was certainly the most foolish gnu in the world. He swallowed hard and mumbled, "Of course, it's a mirror. I was playing a little joke on you."

The guru didn't believe him, but he said, "Never mind. I've pounced all over this cloud and there's no gatekeeper and no gate. It's the wrong cloud."

"But that's impossible. It has to be the right cloud. On our trip to the castle, we saw only one cloud and that was the one with the gate in it. This has to be the right cloud."

"I can't help that," said the guru. "There is no gate in this cloud. This cloud is full of mirrors. So let's get out of here and be on our way."

"How?" said the gnu, who was still terribly depressed.

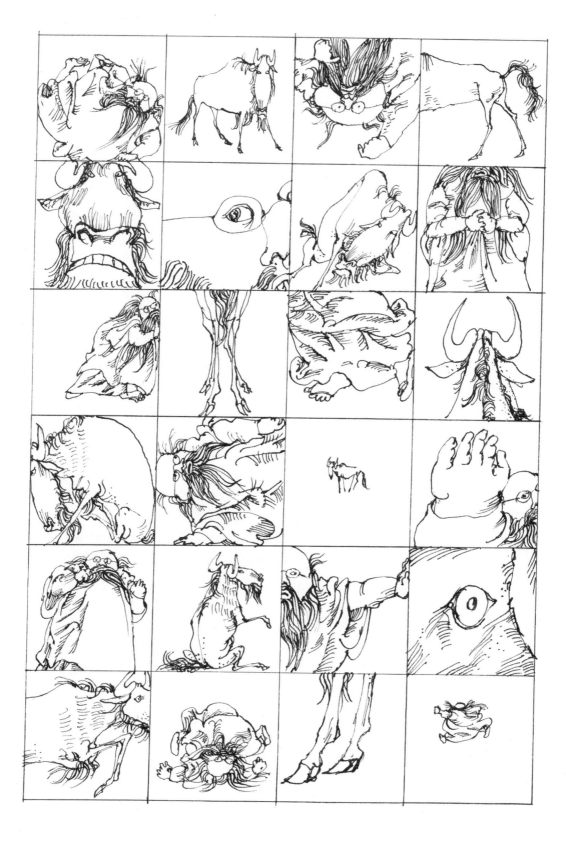

"How what?" said the guru.

"How do we get out of this cloud?"

"Follow me," said the guru. "I've pounced all over this cloud. I know it inside and out." At that point, he pounced right into a mirror. "OUCH!"

"It's not as easy as it looks, is it?" said the gnu, stifling a laugh.

"I guess not. Besides that, crashing into yourself is very disconcerting. It's like watching yourself slip on a banana peel. It's very bad for the morale." The guru rubbed his back, as he got up.

The gnu said, "Let's go this way." Stepping confidently forward, he walked right into himself. There were mirrors all around them. "This is very frustrating," he said. "Let's go this way." Again, he bumped into himself. "What a silly mess this is! Imprisoned by mirrors. After all we've been through today, it doesn't seem fair."

The gnu and the guru wandered, pounced, and bounced around in the cloudful of mirrors for almost an hour. Once, the gnu saw twelve other gnus. A few minutes later, the guru saw twenty-four of himself. But, finally, the gnu took one long, last leap and landed outside the cloud, on the neatly trimmed grass. Afraid to go back into the cloud, he guided the guru out with voice signals.

Once out of the cloud, the guru collapsed on the ground. "That was exhausting. Exhausting! I shall never look in another mirror as long as I live. I've seen enough of myself in the last hour to last me a lifetime. It's true, you know."

"What?"

"They have harnessed the clouds," the guru replied.

"Sad, isn't it?"

The guru got wearily to his feet and they set out again. After walking for a few minutes, they came to a very orderly little hill. "Let's go up this hill," said the gnu. "I remember something about a hill when we were being taken to the castle."

"Yes. So do I," said the gnu. "Let's go."

They walked up the little hill and down the other side. It was precisely twenty-seven steps up and twenty-seven steps down for the gnu and thirty-five up and thirty-five down for the guru. And there, on the other side of the hill, was another cloud.

"Surely, that's the cloud with the gate in it," said the gnu.

"Perhaps," said the guru. "But let's be more careful this time. I'd hate to end up in another cloudful of mirrors. You know, we spent about an hour in the last cloud. The Ugga-Wuggas are certain to have discovered that we've escaped by now. They're probably already looking for us."

"Yes. What'll we do?"

"This time we'll just stroll slowly and quietly into the cloud. That way we can back right out if it's the wrong cloud."

"All right," said the gnu.

The gnu and the guru strolled slowly and quietly up to the cloud, paused, and walked in. They strolled right onto the great paddle wheel of a giant steamboat and it whirled them through the water, through the air, and flung them right back out of the cloud into the meadow before they knew what was happening.

"That wasn't the right cloud either," said the gnu, as he wrung the water out of his tail.

"No," said the guru. "That was definitely not the right cloud." He stood up and began squeezing the water out of his robes.

"What was that?" asked the gnu, shaking himself dry in the warm night air.

"A great paddle wheeler. I haven't seen one in years," said the guru, as he wrung out his beard.

"What was it doing in that cloud?"

"I have no idea. These harnessed clouds are exceedingly, well, unpredictable."

"Odd, too."

"Perhaps not. Perhaps they are normal clouds. Perhaps the clouds we see in the skies at home have things like mirrors and paddle-wheelers in them, too," said the guru.

"Perhaps. Almost nothing would surprise me now. Do you think we could rest for a little while? That trip on that awful wheel thing exhausted me," said the gnu.

"It was actually a very short trip. It couldn't have lasted for more than a minute," said the guru.

"Yes, but it was such a surprise, such a shock. Shocks and surprises always tire me out. And I've had more shocks and surprises today than I've had in my entire life," said the gnu miserably.

"I agree, but I think we'd better keep going. We must find the right cloud. We must escape," said the guru, sounding very tired himself.

"I suppose you're right. I'll have plenty of time to rest at home, assuming, of course, that we ever get home. I've decided not to go to France after all," said the gnu.

Squeezing two final drops of water out of his beard, the guru nodded. "Traveling is very unsettling. Shall we go?"

"I guess so," said the gnu, shaking his head. "I think I have some water in my ear."

"What does it feel like?"

"It feels like I have water in my ear."

"Oh."

"Exactly."

"Well, let's move along," said the guru.

"All right. But I hope the next cloud is, well, friendlier."

"I wouldn't count on it."

"I'm not counting on it, just hoping," said the gnu.

"In fact, we should have a plan for the next cloud."

"I agree. But the thing about these clouds is that you can't see into them and, once inside, you can't see anything at all. And it's very hard to make a really good plan when you can't see where you're going."

"Yes. It's rather like trying to wrestle a bear blindfolded," said the guru.

"Have you ever wrestled a bear blindfolded?" asked the gnu.

"No. Have you?"

"No."

"Oh."

"But that's what it's like," said the guru.

"I think I'd prefer the bear and the blindfold."

"Well, each to his own. Let's get on with it."

Side by side, the gnu and the guru walked through the dark, eyes darting in every direction. Their enthusiasm for breaching clouds had diminished completely. It was obvious by now that finding the right cloud, the one with the gate in it, would be exceedingly difficult and perhaps impossible. The night was quiet and apparently serene and the gnu and the guru crept through the quiet with the stealth of black cats on Halloween.

"Don't you think it's odd that there aren't any birds here?" whispered the guru.

"I think everything here is odd," said the gnu. "Birds are probably too untidy for the Ugga-Wuggas. Flying about, singing when they feel like it. Besides, wheeling and dipping through the air as they do, they would probably scratch the sky."

"I've always thought birds were exceptionally neat myself," said the guru.

"You have different standards," said the gnu.

"That I do," sighed the guru. "Look! Another cloud!"

A great fat cloud was shimmering in front of them.

"Where did it come from?" asked the gnu. "It wasn't there a minute ago."

"They're anything but trustworthy, these clouds," said the guru. "But I suppose we'd better look inside."

"Shall we stroll or pounce into this one?" asked the gnu.

"I really don't think that it makes much difference," said the guru. "Let's get it over with. A flying leap might be fitting at this juncture."

"All right. A flying leap it is. On your mark, get set, GO," shouted the gnu.

The gnu and the guru ran at the cloud and leapt into it without looking to right or left.

"OUCH!" shouted the gnu, landing on his head. "Where are we? What is it? Is there a gate?"

"I don't know about you," answered the guru, "But I seem to be on a merry-go-round."

"How nice," said the gnu. "I've never been on a merry-go-round before. Shall we have a little ride before we press on?"

"I don't think we have a choice," said the guru, clutching on to a wooden horse's tail.

The gnu tried to stand up and was flung back to the floor by the speed of the merry-go-round. "I'm getting dizzy," he said.

"So am I," said the guru. "As long as we're here, let's enjoy ourselves. You take that purple horse and I'll take this yellow one."

"All right," said the gnu. "I like this much better than either the mirrors or the paddle wheel." As he climbed up onto the purple horse and grasped the reins, it turned around and bit him on the nose. The gnu, screaming with pain, leapt off the horse and cried, "He bit me! He bit me! Right on the nose!"

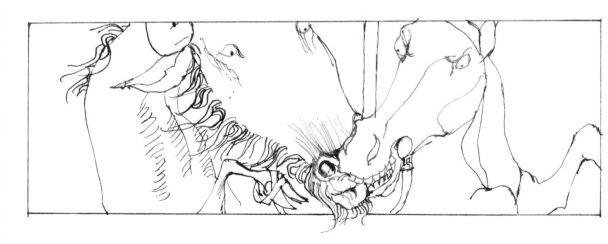

"That's ridiculous," said the guru, who was climbing onto the yellow horse. "Merry-go-round horses can't bite. They're wooden."

"Wooden or not, he bit me! Nasty creature. I should have known this was too good to be true."

The guru yelped and flung himself off the yellow horse. "You're right! You're right! They do bite!"

"I don't like to say I told you so, but I told you so." Trying to maintain his balance on the spinning disc and, simultaneously, trying to avoid the snapping teeth of the horses, the gnu edged his way over to the guru. "Now what?"

"We'd better whisper, the horses are definitely not on our side," said the guru. "I think we'd better get out of here. It's clear that we are quite unwelcome."

"You mean jump off?"

"I mean jump off. Immediately."

"But we might break something . . . a leg, our heads. Both," whispered the gnu.

"We'll have to chance it. Actually, I think I'd rather break a leg than stay here and be nipped to death by these horses."

"I agree . . . I guess," said the gnu. "Only I have twice as many legs to break as you do." He scratched his head. "All right. Let's go,"

They crept to the edge of the merry-go-round and, just as they were about to jump off, they were picked up and lifted back to the center by the yellow horse and the purple horse. The gnu was furious.

"I'm furious," he said. "You'd think that if they disliked us enough to bite us, they'd simply let us go and be done with it."

"Obviously, they are very contrary," said the guru.

Once again, the gnu and the guru crept to the edge and once again they were lifted back to the center by the horses.

"That's not funny!" shouted the gnu.

"No, it's a very bad joke," said the guru.

Four times they crept to the edge and four times they were lifted back to the center by the wooden horses. By this time, the gnu was in an uncontrollable rage, kicking and biting and shouting. But the horses remained calm.

"Whatever I do, I can't seem to upset the horses," he said angrily.

"Of course not. They're wooden." He whispered in the gnu's ear. "We'll have to take them by surprise. We'll have to charge. Charge right through them and off the edge."

"But I'm tired and dizzy. I'm not sure I'm up to a charge," sighed the gnu.

"Do you want to stay here?"

"I'm up to a charge."

"All right. Let's go. NOW!" The gnu and the guru charged through the horses and leapt off the merry-go-round.

"It worked!" shouted the gnu, as he rolled rapidly down a hill.

"So it did!" answered the gnu, who was rolling rapidly down the hill, too.

Colliding at the bottom of the hill, the gnu and the guru sat up and shook their heads.

"Good grief!" said the gnu. "I'm seeing double."

"It'll pass. You're just dizzy."

"I hope so," sighed the gnu. "Are any of my legs broken?"

"I don't know. They don't look broken."

"I guess I'm all right then. These clouds are getting worse and worse. If we don't find the one with the gate in it soon, there'll be nothing left of us," said the gnu.

"I'm losing interest in the search," said the guru.

"But we can't give up. We must keep going. Otherwise we'll never get out. We'll be here forever. And there's no telling what the Ugga-Wuggas will do to us if they catch us again. After all, escaped prisoners aren't neat," said the gnu.

"Or orderly."

"Or tidy."

"You're right, Gnu. Let's go."

The guru stood up and the gnu followed him. By now, both were limping. Indeed, they were a pathetic sight, hobbling through the dark, groaning quietly.

"We must be a pathetic sight," said the gnu.

"Yes," answered the guru. They walked, silent and forlorn, for quite a while before they saw another cloud. Suddenly, there it was, right in front of them.

"There's another cloud," said the gnu without enthusiasm. "Shall we have a go at it?"

"Yes. Pouncing's no good, neither is strolling. Let's charge."

"Why not? I couldn't feel worse."

"On your mark, get set, GO," shouted the guru, and they charged. Luckily, because they were hurt and tired, they weren't up to a really first-rate charge.

Flattened by the cloud, the gnu lay on the ground. "I'd swear that cloud hit me," he said.

"Yes," replied the guru, who also found himself on the ground, "It hit me, too." He got slowly to his feet and approached the cloud cautiously. "This cloud is made of stone! No wonder it knocked us silly."

"How marvelous!"

"What do you mean?" asked the guru.

"Well, after the clouds we've been through, I find a stone cloud so simple, so direct, so, well, old-fashioned."

"But it's an incredible contradiction. Stone is heavy and solid. Clouds are light and airy. Isn't it therefore amazing to find a stone cloud?" asked the guru.

"No. You are amazing," said the gnu.

"Thank you. But why?" said the guru, obviously pleased.

"You are amazing because you can go through a cloud filled with mirrors, a cloud with a huge paddle-wheeler in it, and a cloud containing a merry-go-round, yet you find a simple stone cloud curious," explained the gnu.

"But don't you see? The other clouds — despite their peculiar contents — were clouds. They were made of air and water, just like other clouds. This cloud is made of stone. In fact, it is the exact opposite of a cloud. Don't you see?"

"Yes, I see," said the gnu. "I simply don't care. I'm tired. I'm hungry. I ache all over. Contradictions and conundrums don't interest me. If I saw a stone made of water and air right now, I wouldn't even pause to examine it."

The guru sighed. "You should be more curious, you know."

"Perhaps. But now I'd like to go home. I'll be curious another day. Let's get on with it."

"All right," said the guru. "But it is a lovely riddle, this stone cloud."

"Let's go, Guru."

Thoroughly exhausted, the gnu and the guru tracked through the dark. The painted sky was slowly filling with light. The night had seemed endless to them, but the beginning of the new day made them move more quickly. They would be easy targets for the Ugga-Wuggas in the daylight. Looking carefully to the right and the left, they pressed onward. Suddenly, there was another cloud in front of them. The very sight made them wince, but they approached it nonetheless.

"Which shall it be?" asked the gnu. "Pouncing, strolling, charging? Which?"

"Let's stroll."

"All right. I'm not up to pouncing or charging anyway," mumbled the gnu.

Tense and nervous, but trying to appear calm and relaxed, the gnu and the guru strolled into the cloud. In a moment, they were enveloped in whiteness. Barely able to see each other, they were unable to see anything else at all. Silently, they tiptoed through the blankness. Then they heard something.

"Oh," shuddered the gnu. "I hope it isn't another merry-go-round. That was the worst of all."

"SSSSH!" said the guru.

"HALT! WHO GOES THERE? WHAT'S THE PASSWORD? FRIEND OR FOE?" The voice boomed through the cloud and frightened the gnu and the guru so much that they fell down.

"Who was that?" said the gnu, clutching onto the guru's arm.

"The gatekeeper!"

"How do you know?" asked the gnu.

"Because he said all those gatekeeper things. 'Halt!' and all that. Where do you suppose he is?" asked the guru.

"You mean this is the right cloud? You mean we've finally found the right cloud?" caroled the gnu.

"Precisely. But now we have to get through the gate. That may be the hardest trick of all," warned the guru.

Again the voice rang through the cloud, "HALT! WHO GOES THERE? WHAT'S THE PASSWORD? FRIEND OR FOE?"

"He sounds very big," said the guru.

"But there are two of us," said the gnu.

"True," said the guru. "Shall we pounce on him?"

"We have to find him first," said the gnu.

"True."

"I think he's over here. Let's creep," said the gnu.

"All right," said the guru. "Shall I go first?"

"That would be grand."

"Here I go. Hold on to my robes."

The gnu and the guru crept, single-file, through the white and, without warning, the guru found himself face-to-face with the gatekeeper. "Good grief!" said the guru.

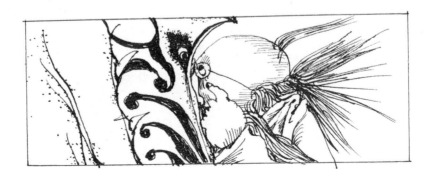

"Who are you?" said the gatekeeper.

"What's going on?" asked the gnu from the white.

"I found the gatekeeper," said the guru.

"Oh," said the gnu.

"HALT! WHO GOES THERE? WHAT'S THE PASSWORD? FRIEND OR FOE?" said the gatekeeper.

"Please," said the guru. "One question at a time. Which would you like me to answer first?"

The gatekeeper thought for a moment. "Well, you've already halted. 'Who goes there?' I guess."

"The gnu and the guru," said the guru.

"Are you a juggling team? I'm very fond of juggling teams?" said the gatekeeper.

"No. Sorry," said the guru.

"What then?" asked the gatekeeper.

"That's not one of the questions. Stick to the questions. The next one is 'what's the password?'"

"Right," said the gatekeeper. "I got carried away. What's the password?"

"Watermelon," said the gnu, who had moved up beside the guru.

"Wrong!" said the guard.

"Rooftop," said the guru.

"Wrong," said the guard.

"We give up," said the gnu. "What is the password?"

"Cataclysm," said the gatekeeper.

"Right! Cataclysm," said the gnu and the guru together.

"All right," said the gnu. "Next question."

"What is the next question?" asked the gatekeeper who, by now, was thoroughly muddled.

"Friend or foe?" said the gnu.

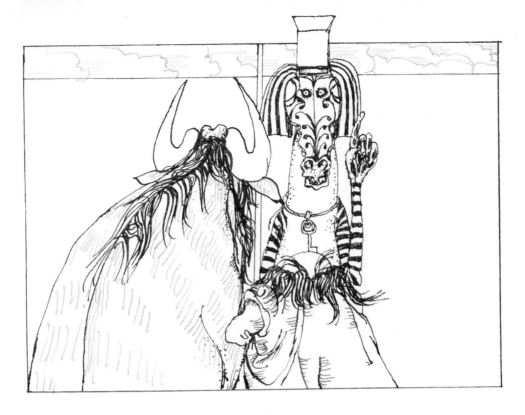

"Right," said the gatekeeper. "Friend or foe?"

"Friend, of course," said the gnu. "After all, if we were foes, we would have chopped off your head by now."

"Oh, my goodness," said the gatekeeper. "Is that what foes do?"

"Where's the regular gatekeeper?" asked the guru.

"Asleep in the gatekeeper's house," said the gate-keeper. He looked at the sky thoughtfully. "He'll be awake in forty-seven minutes. Would you like to wait?"

"Oh, we'd like to. We'd like to very much. But we can't. You see, we have very pressing business. We must be on our way. So if you'll be good enough to open the gate, we'll be going," said the guru as firmly and confidently as possible.

"I can't do that," said the gatekeeper.

"Why not?" asked the guru. "You're the gate-keeper."

"But I'm only an apprentice gatekeeper. Apprentice gatekeepers can't actually open the gate. They can stand by the gate and say 'HALT!' and all those other things, but they can't actually open the gate. I'm sorry, but you'll have to wait until the master gate-keeper wakes up." He looked at the sky again. "Only forty-six minutes now."

"But we can't wait," said the guru. "I told you, we have very pressing business. We can't afford to be late."

"I don't know about that," said the gatekeeper. "I only know that I'm not allowed to open the gate. If the leader himself appeared, I couldn't open it."

"Would he have to wait until the master gatekeeper woke up?" asked the gnu.

"Of course not. He could open the gate himself. After all, he's a very important person. You can't keep him waiting," said the gatekeeper respectfully.

"Well, my friend, we're very important, too. So we'll just open the gate ourselves," said the guru.

The gatekeeper moved between the gate and the guru. "No, you can't do that. Only leaders can do that."

"Well, in my fashion, I'm a leader."

"You are?" asked the gatekeeper.

"Indeed."

"Well, in that case . . . No, I can't do it. I'm terribly sorry," said the gatekeeper.

"Why not?" asked the guru.

"It's against the rules."

"My good fellow, rules are made to be broken," said the guru with impressive authority.

"I didn't know that," said the gatekeeper.

"Absolutely! Isn't that right, Gnu?"

"Absolutely."

The gatekeeper frowned and scratched his chin. "No, I don't think so. I'm sorry, but I'm only an apprentice. Apprentices aren't allowed to make decisions," said the gatekeeper.

"By the way," said the gnu, "do you have a spear?"

"Yes, I do," said the gatekeeper.

"Might I look at it? I'm a great admirer of spears," said the gnu.

"Of course. It's an awfully nice one. My father gave it to me," the gatekeeper said proudly.

"Indeed? Let me see it," said the gnu in a very friendly way.

The young gatekeeper handed his spear over to the gnu.

Holding it, the gnu said, "Nice. Very nice. This is one of the nicest spears I've ever seen." Without warning, he thrust the blade of the spear at the gate-keeper's neck, pinning him against the gate.

"What are you doing?" asked the frightened gate-keeper.

"Testing your spear, of course. And if you aren't very quiet and if you don't hand over the key to the gate, I'll have to test it in a more dramatic fashion. Do you understand, Gatekeeper?"

"You mean you'll chop off my head?" said the gate-keeper.

"Precisely. Now, the key please," said the gnu.

"You aren't a friend at all. You're a foe. You cheated," moaned the gatekeeper.

"Of course we're your friends. We simply do not have time to wait for the master gatekeeper to wake up.

We have an important appointment to keep. Now . . .
the key, please," said the gnu.

"You've hurt my feelings," said the gatekeeper.

"THE KEY!" said the gnu again.

The gatekeeper handed over the key and said sadly,
"What about my feelings?"

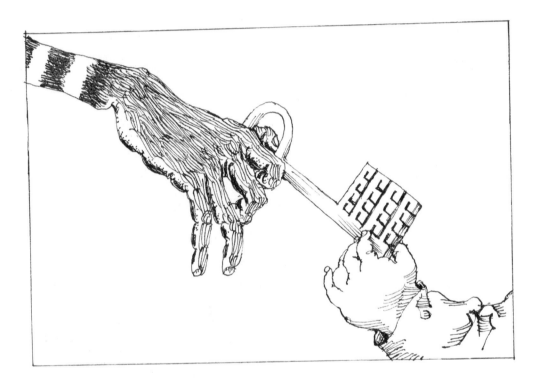

"I'm sorry about that. But it's been a very long
night. Well, goodbye and good luck. Shall we go,
Guru?"

They unlocked the gate with the golden key and
stepped through. Then they closed it behind them.
They were out. They were free. It seemed such a simple
act, opening and closing a gate, but it overjoyed them
beyond reason.

They did a spontaneous little jig. "We're out!" they shouted. "We're free!" they called. "We made it!" they said. And did another little jig.

"Look!" cried the guru. "There's my bike. Right where I left it."

"Let's get on it and ride away from here immediately," said the gnu.

"Good idea," said the guru.

They got on the bike and the guru pedaled furiously and, in a moment, they were out of the cloud and away from the Behind-the-Beyond.

"We're out! We're free! We're out! We're free!" they sang as they whirled along.

"Doesn't everything look wonderful?" asked the guru. "Isn't it grand?"

"Wonderful!" shouted the gnu. "Beautiful! Look at that beautiful meadow full of weeds and wild flowers."

"Look at those shaggy, bushy trees!"

"Look at those glorious ruts in the road!"

"Look at that glorious dirt!"

"Look at that splendid streaky sky!"

"Look at those fluffy white clouds!"

"I hate clouds," said the gnu.

"You can't go around hating clouds for the rest of your life. Let's make a rule. Clouds in the sky are fine. Clouds on the ground are something else again," said the guru, pleased with his own wisdom.

"All right. I guess that's reasonable enough. There's a stream. I'm awfully thirsty. Shall we stop?" asked the gnu.

"Yes. That's a grand idea. We can rest, too. I'm awfully tired," said the guru. They stopped at the stream and drank.

Looking at himself in the water, the gnu said, "I don't look the least bit different. I look just the same. Back there, in the Behind-the-Beyond, I thought I might have changed."

"You sound disappointed."

"I am. A little bit anyway. After all, gnus aren't the most beautiful beasts in the world."

"But you have a very good heart," said the guru.

"Thank you. My, I'm awfully tired. I think I'll take a little nap," said the gnu.

"That's a good idea."

They both went to sleep immediately and slept for several hours in the sun. On waking, the guru nudged the gnu. "I had a most peculiar dream about a place called the Behind-the-Beyond. The trees were square and the sky was painted on and the clouds were full of surprises. You were in the dream, too."

"That wasn't a dream. It actually happened," said the gnu.

"Are you sure?" said the guru.